# The Lion and the Mouse

Retold by Cheyenne Cisco
Illustrated by John Manders

**Sadlier-Oxford**
A Division of William H. Sadlier, Inc.
New York, NY 10005-1002

A big, bossy lion and a quiet, little mouse lived side by side in the jungle.

2

"Me, myself, and I!" roared the lion.
"I'm the best! I'm the boss! I am king
of this jungle!"
Oh, was he noisy!

3

The lion yelled and shouted until he tired himself out. Then he lay down and closed his eyes. Soon the big, bossy lion was fast asleep.

Along came the quiet, little mouse.
He saw a fat berry up in the bush.
"Yummy!" he whispered to himself.
"But I'd better not wake that lion."

5

The mouse crept closer. He could
almost taste that berry. He didn't see
when one big, lion eye opened.
The lion was awake!

Bam! The lion's huge, hairy paw came
down on the mouse's bald, pink tail.
"Got you!" the lion yelled.

Then the lion bent down near the tiny mouse.
"Mmm," he said, "a tasty, little snack for lunch."

8

"No!" begged the mouse.
"I'm too skinny to eat! Please
let me go. Maybe I'll help
you one day."

9

"Ha! Ha!" laughed the lion. "I am king of this jungle. You're just a little mouse. You could never help me."

10

"Yes, I could! You never know when
you'll need a friend," said the mouse.
The lion took his paw off the mouse.
"Go away and stay away," said the lion.

That night, the lion got into a jam.
"I'm the best! I'm the boss!" he boasted.
But the lion didn't watch where he was
going. Swish!

12

"Help! Help!" the lion cried.
"I'll end up in the zoo!"
And from far away, the quiet,
little mouse heard the loud lion.

13

The mouse ran to the trap as fast as he could. He began to chew on the big, fat ropes.

14

At last, the little mouse set the lion free!
"Thanks, pal," said the lion. "I will always
remember what you did for me."

Be nice!
You never know
who your next
friend will be.